Meet . . .

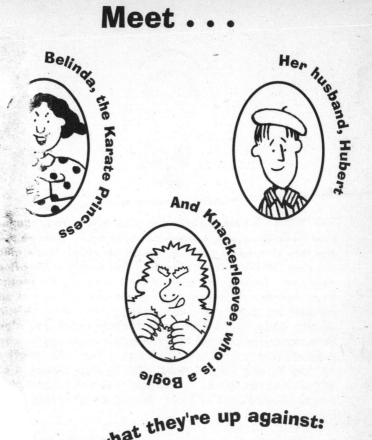

Belinda, the Karate Princess

Her husband, Hubert

And Knackerleevee, who is a Bogle

And this is what they're up against:

a rather t

Nsta . . .

Jeremy Strong once worked in a bakery, putting the jam into three thousand doughnuts every night. Now he puts the jam in stories instead, which he finds much more exciting. At the age of three, he fell out of a first-floor bedroom window and landed on his head. His mother says that this damaged him for the rest of his life and refuses to take any responsibility. He loves writing stories because he says it is 'the only time you alone have complete control and can make anything happen'. His ambition is to make you laugh (or at least snuffle). Jeremy Strong lives in Kent with his wife, Susan, a cat or two, and something in the attic that makes scratching noises at night, but he hasn't found out what it is yet.

Some other books by Jeremy Strong

DINOSAUR POX

THE HUNDRED-MILE-AN-HOUR DOG

MY GRANNY'S GREAT ESCAPE

THE KARATE PRINCESS
THE KARATE PRINCESS AND THE
CUT-THROAT ROBBERS
THE KARATE PRINCESS TO THE RESCUE
THE KARATE PRINCESS AND THE LAST GRIFFIN

Jeremy Strong

The Karate Princess in MoNsta Trouble

PUFFIN BOOKS

PUFFIN BOOKS

Published by the Penguin Group
Penguin Books Ltd, 80 Strand, London WC2R 0RL, England
Penguin Putnam Inc., 375 Hudson Street, New York, New York 10014, USA
Penguin Books Australia Ltd, 250 Camberwell Road, Camberwell, Victoria 3124, Australia
Penguin Books Canada Ltd, 10 Alcorn Avenue, Toronto, Ontario, Canada M4V 3B2
Penguin Books India (P) Ltd, 11 Community Centre, Panchsheel Park, New Delhi – 110 017, India
Penguin Books (NZ) Ltd, Cnr Rosedale and Airborne Roads, Albany, Auckland, New Zealand
Penguin Books (South Africa) (Pty) Ltd, 24 Sturdee Avenue, Rosebank 2196, South Africa

Penguin Books Ltd, Registered Offices: 80 Strand, London WC2R 0RL, England

www.penguin.com

First published by A & C Black 1999
Published in Puffin Books 2001
8

Text copyright © Jeremy Strong, 1999
Illustrations copyright © Rowan Clifford, 2001
Illustrations based on the original artwork of Nick Sharratt © Nick Sharratt, 2001
All rights reserved

The moral right of the author has been asserted

Set in Baskerville MT 14/19

Made and printed in England by Clays Ltd, St Ives plc

British Library Cataloguing in Publication Data
A CIP catalogue record for this book is available from the British Library

ISBN 0-141-30492-8

1 A Very Interesting Letter

The sun was shining, the sky was blue, the summer leaves were green, and the peaceful silence of the countryside was only broken by the sound of singing.

'. . . Ziss leetle boat, sail, sail away, wizzer princess and high majesty . . .'

Up and down went the raspy, wheezing voice, as sweet and tender as sandpaper. It was a curious sound, and it came from a curious person. He was large and powerfully built, with long arms, long fingers and even longer fingernails. He had sharp, white teeth. He had flaring nostrils and red eyes. And more than anything else, he was hairy. He had hair everywhere, including the soles of his feet.

Although the noise

made by this strange creature sounded like a weasel being hit on the head, in fact he was singing. He was happy. He was singing for Belinda, the Karate Princess, and her very new husband, Hubert. Hubert and Belinda were on their honeymoon, and they had taken their best friend Knackerleevee with them.

It was Knackerleevee who was singing, in his best Bogle fashion. Knackerleevee was a Bogle of course, and that's why he was so big and strong and hairy. He was also a wee bit smelly, although he didn't pong quite so much since Belinda's mum (the Queen) had given him some aftershave for Christmas.

And now all three of them were drifting down the river, gazing up at the beautiful blue sky, and the chirping birds, and the fliffy-fluffy clouds, and the itty-pretty . . .

'I'm going mad with boredom!' Belinda suddenly yelled at the sky. 'I can't take any more of this mooning about doing nothing except admiring scenery and saying what lovely weather it is. If something interesting doesn't happen soon I shall, I shall, I shall . . .

2

urgh!' Belinda gave a desperate grunt, leapt from her seat and threw herself overboard. There was a loud splash and she vanished.

'Woman overboard!' cried Knackerleevee. 'Her Highshipnest is drowning!' The Bogle began rowing rapidly in as many different directions as possible in a frantic search for Belinda, but all that could be seen was a trail of bubbles on the surface.

Hubert leaned anxiously over the side, peering into the water. All at once a hand shot out of the water, grabbed the side of the boat and wrenched it so fiercely that both Knackerleevee and

Hubert were cast into the water themselves.

Belinda surfaced, laughing loudly, but the Bogle was struggling and making strange gurgling noises.

'Ug, ug, I can't cug ug

urgurgle gurgle SWIM!' he finally managed to spurt out, along with a mouthful of river water and two very surprised fish.

'You are hopeless,' muttered Belinda as she grasped hold of the Bogle's hairy head and held him above the water. With Hubert's help she got Knackerleevee to the shore, where he lay in a soggy heap, panting.

'I had to stop you singing somehow,' Belinda explained. 'Anyway, you used to live in The Marsh at the End of the World – the wettest place on earth – so how come you can't swim?'

'You don't swim in a marsh,' growled Knackerleevee. 'It's not deep enough. If it was deep it wouldn't be a marsh, it would be a lake.'

Belinda grinned at him cheerfully. 'I suppose that makes sense,' she admitted. 'Well, now what shall we do?' she asked, looking at her two friends for ideas.

'I'm wet,' said Hubert. 'Why don't we go back home so we can put dry clothes on?'

'I think her Royal Majesticbit will have to hang me on the washing line,' said

Knackerleevee gloomily. 'It will take me weeks to dry out.'

'Don't be such a pair of miseries. It's only water. In fact it was fun. It was the best fun we've had since the wedding. We've been here two days – TWO DAYS – and done absolutely nothing. I need action. There must be something to do.'

'We could get dry,' chorused Hubert and the Bogle. 'That would be something to do.'

Belinda looked at them both and sighed. They were wet all over and limp round the

edges. She had to admit they did look just a little bit bedraggled. 'All right, we'll go home. Honestly, you two must be the wettest wets in the whole kingdom.'

'Thank you, Your Majesty,' said Hubert, a trifle coldly.

'Come on, I'll race you both!' Belinda cried and shot off across the grass towards her father's castle.

'Not running as well,' moaned Knackerleevee, watching the fast vanishing princess. 'I hate running with wet fur. It slaps around too much. Honestly, first I almost drown and now I have to slap myself with my own fur.'

'She's bored,' Hubert explained. 'She needs an adventure. I do hope she manages to find something to do soon.'

'Me too, as long as it isn't too far away, or too dangerous, or involves drowning and running. Come on, we'd better try and catch her up.'

By the time Hubert and Knackerleevee reached King Stormbelly's castle, Belinda was already trying to use up her surplus energy. She was pacing up and down the veranda, beheading various ancient members of the royal family as she went. Fortunately this was not quite as dreadful as it sounds – they weren't real members of the family – they were statues that were placed all along the veranda. However, the princess's father, King Stormbelly, found it a trifle annoying.

'I do wish you wouldn't use your karate around the castle,' he grumbled. 'You do realize that you've just chopped off your Great Uncle Albert's head? And there goes Auntie Rosie! Can't you find anything better to do?'

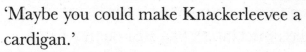

'You should try knitting, dear,' said the Queen equably. 'Maybe you could make Knackerleevee a cardigan.'

'A cardigan?!' Belinda burst out laughing.

'Or a pair of socks,' added the Queen, ignoring her daughter's loud snorts.

'You can't ask a great big hairy Bogle to wear a cardigan and socks!'

At this moment Knackerleevee appeared on the veranda. He stared sheepishly at the floor and twiddled his long fingernails.

'Actually, Your Worshipness, I would rather like a cardigan, I think . . . and socks. I've never had a cardigan or socks before.' The Bogle raised his sad eyes and gazed wistfully at the Queen.

'Oh, Knackerleevee – I didn't realize! I mean, I never thought – I shall knit you a cardigan at once. Come over here so I can measure your arms, and tell me what colour you'd like.' The Bogle immediately perked up and hurried over to the Queen, while Belinda threw herself into a deckchair and watched them moodily.

'I cannot believe that a great big hairy Bogle could get excited about a-a-a cardigan,' she snapped. 'And socks!' She spat out the words as if they were highly poisonous.

Hubert smiled. 'He's spent most of his life in a rather wet, rather gloomy, rather miserable marsh. A cardigan must seem quite splendid to him.'

Belinda turned and looked up at her husband. Her eyes filled with tenderness. 'That's why I married you. Oh, Hubert, I know I can be horrible at times. I only think of myself and adventures. You're quite right of course. Cardigans and socks must seem very exciting to someone who's lived in a soggy marsh. It's just that . . .' her voice trailed away. 'I wish there was something really exciting to do.'

Hubert squeezed her hand. 'It would be good. You could have an adventure, and I could paint it.'

At this moment there was a loud clatter from

beyond and a lot of shouting. A messenger
came galloping round the side of the castle,
skidded to a halt and was thrown head-over-
heels from his panting pony, landing in a cloud
of dust at King Stormbelly's feet. The
messenger plucked a letter from his pocket and
waved it at the King.

'Urgent message from my master, the Duke,'
he cried.

'Oh! A letter. How fascinating.' The King
pushed a podgy finger under the seal and
unrolled the battered scroll. 'Ah! It's from my
brother!'

'Which brother is that, dear?' enquired the
Queen, knowing that the King had
seven brothers dotted about
here and there.

'It's Dudless, Duke of
Dork,' began
Stormbelly, straining his
eyes to read the childlike
scrawl. The Queen was
surprised.

'Really? I didn't think

Dudless could read, let alone write.'

'It is an odd letter,' admitted King Stormbelly. He showed it to Belinda. 'There – what do you make of it?'

Belinda studied the message carefully.

A slow smile spread across Belinda's face. 'At last,' she sighed dreamily. 'An adventure – something to do. Hurrah.'

Dear BroTha,
Pleze help. Wee aRR been ~~Tebbaw Jerry Teltokyd~~ TERRoRyzed by A MoNsta. IT haz got 1 TaLe, 2 HedZ, 4 TuNgZ, 2 wiNgZ and 4 leggZ. IT goez RAAArgh! aNd Maks us RuN away (veRRyfAst) Becoz if IT catcHes ANywuN iT EETsTHEM! It haz Eaten My ArMee aNd My peT raBBiT ToNy. We doNt lik iT verry MucH. But we're scaREdy kats so PlESE HELPp. SeND yor verry bestest MaN.
P.S. THeRe is a prise foR tHe peRsuN who ~~spifffle~~ spifflykates tHe MoNsta
Luv and kiSSEz
Dudless, Duck of DoRk

2 Introducing Dudless, Duke of Dork

'Come on!' cried the Karate Princess. 'There's a two-headed MoNsta on the loose, eating armies and pet rabbits. And there's a prize too – so hurry up!'

'But what about my cardigan?' Knackerleevee was crestfallen.

The Queen patted Knackerleevee on one hairy arm. 'It's all right, dear, you run along. I've got all the measurements I need. By the time you get back I might even have finished it.'

'Now look here,' steamed King Stormbelly, 'you're on your honeymoon. You're supposed to be relaxing.'

'If I relax any more my head will fall off.'

'I do wish you were more like your other sisters. I mean to say, they're all . . .'

'Beautiful?' suggested Belinda.

'Exactly. And they're . . .'

'Witty?' Belinda put in.

'Quite so. And they're . . .'

'Boring?' said Belinda slyly.

'Definitely! Heh – no! I mean definitely not! You-you,' stuttered the King, 'you were trying to trick me then, weren't you?'

Belinda gave her father an innocent glance. The Queen laughed quietly. 'I think you must admit dear that your youngest daughter is every bit as clever as her sisters – if not cleverer.'

'Doh! Codswallop and poppywhatsits. If you want to go dancing off to get chewed up by a two-headed MoNsta then don't expect me to stop you.'

'But you are trying to stop me,' Belinda pointed out.

'Ah! Ah!' cried the King, wagging a finger at his daughter. 'I was, but I'm not any longer, and I hope he eats you up in one mouthful. See if I care!'

'Thank you, Daddy.' Belinda smiled, kissing her father on his bald head and making him blush furiously. 'I shall take that as your blessing on our dangerous mission. Come on, Hubert. You'd better go and pack all your paint things.'

So it was that a short time later the three adventurers climbed on to their horses (Knackerleevee's horse was an extra large, extra strong beast called Goliath), and set off to find Stormbelly's brother and the dreadful MoNsta.

Hubert was carrying a big, sharp sword. Knackerleevee was also armed to the teeth. (Actually he was armed *with* his teeth – and his long talons and great strength.) But the only weapon that Belinda had was her bare hands.

Belinda was not known as the Karate Princess for nothing. She had been taught karate by Hiro Ono, the most famous karate expert in this book – even in the whole world, and she had been his best pupil. In fact, so good was Belinda at karate that she had defeated (in the past, and not all at the same time) the merciless Cut-Throat Robbers, a fearful steam-dragon, and a whole army of sumo-wrestlers, not to mention the odious Grand Oompah of Pomposity.

Of course being good at karate was not always quite enough to get by on, but luckily Belinda was also cunning, and she had her two very good companions, Hubert and Knackerleevee, to help her. Now, as they approached her uncle's castle, she had high hopes for an excellent adventure.

The Duke of Dork looked much like his brother Stormbelly, except that he was shorter, fatter, balder and had a very high squeaky voice. This made him seem even more stupid than he really was, and in reality the Duke of Dork was very stupid indeed. He was so useless that Belinda felt quite sorry for him. 'Dorinda!' cried the Duke. 'It's you!'

'BELINDA,' corrected the Karate Princess. 'You always call me Dorinda, and my name is Belinda.'

'Sorry, so sorry. What a wonderful funeral that was! I did enjoy myself. Lovely dress!' The

Duke gave Knackerleevee a sly prod. 'This
must be your new wife? Charming, but a bit
too hairy for my taste, and far too tall. Guard!
Fetch me a ladder so that I can kiss the bride.'
Knackerleevee shot an alarmed look at the
princess.

'It was my WEDDING, Uncle, not a
funeral. And please meet Hubert, my
HUSBAND, who is not at all hairy.'

'Oh silly me, of course. Well, my dears, it is
lovely to see you. Are you on your jammy?'

The three friends glanced at each other.
What was a jammy? The Duke observed their

puzzlement. 'Oh you must know what I mean,' he said airily. 'Maybe I've got the word wrong. I know it's something to do with jam, or is it marmalade? Honey, maybe?'

'Perhaps you mean "honeymoon", ' suggested Hubert politely.

'Of course, yes, that's the one. Is that why you're here? Are you going to spend some of your honeyspoon with us? Splendid!' The Duke of Dork beamed at the Duchess, who Belinda suddenly realized was sitting very quietly in a corner, playing cards with herself.

Belinda hadn't noticed her at all. She hadn't taken part in any of the conversation so far, which Belinda thought was a little strange. Then she remembered that the Duchess always put large chunks of cheese in her ear, as ear plugs, so that she didn't have to listen to her husband's constant nonsense.

'Actually,' said Belinda, 'we've come on another matter.'

'Oh yes? Is it teatime? Have you come for tea?'

'No, Uncle. We haven't come for tea. It's something altogether more dangerous.'

'Ah!' The Duke's eyes lit up. 'Of course! You mean supper. You've come for supper!'

Hubert leaned forward, looking puzzled. 'Is supper dangerous around these parts?' he asked. The Duke nodded seriously.

'Indeed it is. I keep poking myself in the eye with my fork. Daft thing, if you ask me. I'd rather use my fingers.'

'Why don't you?' suggested Hubert. The Duke of Dork took a step back, gazed at Hubert with utter astonishment, stepped forward again, flung his short arms round the painter and hugged him.

'Of course! Why didn't I think of that? Excellent

idea! Oho, I can't wait for supper now, especially if you're coming too.'

'We haven't come for supper,' Belinda explained patiently. 'Don't you remember, Uncle? You wrote to my father about a problem you have here – a big problem.'

'The downstairs toilet doesn't flush any more?'

'No, it wasn't the toilet.'

'It's that mouse in the kitchen, isn't it – the one that keeps eating the Duchess's best Camembert?'

'No, it's not the mouse in the kitchen.'

'Oh.' The Duke gave her a grumpy glance. 'Well, I don't know then. Give me a clue.'

Knackerleevee sighed impatiently.

'It's got two heads and goes "Raaaargh!" ' he growled.

'It's the cat!' cried the Duke with a huge smile.

'NO!' yelled Belinda, finally losing all patience. 'It's the two-headed MoNsta that's eaten your army and your rabbit.'

The Duke of Dork turned very pale and

began to tremble, and since he was mostly
made of fat he trembled quite
spectacularly. His three
chins wobbled, his
cheeks quivered, his
bottom bounced
about and his belly
shook like an
enormous jelly.

'Sssssh! It might hear you.'

'Is it near by?' whispered
Knackerleevee. The Duke shook his head.
'Then why do we have to be quiet?' The Duke
thought about this, his forehead frowning more
and more with each passing second. At last he
shook his head.

'I don't know,' he admitted. 'Could you ask
me again tomorrow, when I've had time to
think about it? I'm afraid I'm rather confused.
I don't understand this at all,' he complained.
'Why are you here?'

'We've come to rid you of the MoNsta,'
Belinda said simply. 'You sent a note to Daddy
asking for help. Well, I'm the help.'

'You?'

'Yes, me and my two friends here, Hubert and Knackerleevee.'

'But, but, you're a princess,' stuttered the Duke.

'Yes.'

'Princesses don't fight MoNstas.'

'Why not?'

'Er, it's um, it's . . .' The poor Duke shook his head again. For several seconds he looked totally stunned, and then a bright thought occurred to him. 'Look here, you can't fight the MoNsta because you can't have the prize.'

'And why can't I have the prize?' asked Belinda.

'Well, it would be so silly, wouldn't it?'

'Why? What is the prize?'

'It's my daughter. Whoever defeats the MoNsta can marry my daughter, Taloola. You can't marry my daughter now, can you?' The Duke beamed at Belinda triumphantly. 'Of course you can't. You're already married!'

The Bogle let out an enormous groan. He was beginning to think it would be a great relief to everyone if the MoNsta did eat the Duke. Belinda gave Hubert a look of despair. She was about to start arguing with the Duke when a door at the far end of the royal chamber burst open and in came Taloola.

At least, she didn't exactly *come* in. It was more like a small explosion of golden hair and red lipstick and mouth and noise and flailing body. Not only was Taloola glamorous, but she was tubby – in fact 'tubular' would probably be a better description. (It was something she had inherited from her father.)

'Popsicle!' cried Taloola, with tears streaming down her face and making rather a mess of her eyeliner and cheek-blush. 'I can't stand any more of this. Everywhere I go there are princes trying to marry me. The castle is full of them! They're even sleeping in cupboards now! I will not marry a handsome prince, not even if the two-headed MoNsta eats everyone in the country; not even if you put sardines in my chocolate mousse; not in a million, zillion years. You know I love Gordon the goatherd, and I shall never marry anyone but him!'

With this magnificent outburst Taloola threw herself howling at her father's feet.

3 Enter the Handsome Prince

It was Hubert who went to
Taloola's rescue. He leaned
over her, crooning gently.
   'There, there,
it's all right,
Taloola
. . . don't
cry.' Then
He made an
almost fatal mistake – he tried to lift Taloola to
her feet. He managed to raise her top half
from the floor, but couldn't manage her legs.
He then succeeded in lifting both her legs, but
couldn't manage her top half. After a couple of
failed attempts he gave Knackerleevee a
desperate look. The Bogle strode over, flung
one arm round Taloola's waist and swept her
from the floor.
   'Oh!' simpered Taloola, fluttering her false
eyelashes at the Bogle. 'You are strong! But

why are you wearing a fur coat? It's the middle of summer. And what's that funny smell?'

'It's not a fur coat. Knackerleevee is a Bogle, and that's his real skin,' Belinda explained.

Taloola gave a startled shriek and hurriedly pulled a pair of glasses from her little handbag. She took one look, slapped the Bogle's face, cried, 'Unhand me, you villainous beast!' and fainted. The Bogle dumped her on the ground and folded his hairy arms.

'I'm not picking her up again,' he growled.

The Duke clapped his hands and four guards appeared. They heaved the unfortunate girl into a seat, where she sat slumped over to one side. Belinda decided that now would be a good opportunity to ask her uncle why the castle was stuffed with princes.

'It's very simple,' explained the Duke. 'The first prince to kill the MoNsta will marry my daughter. You wouldn't believe how many princes have turned up. The castle is crawling with them.'

'And have the princes seen Taloola?' Belinda couldn't help asking.

'Of course,' said the Duke. 'They love her, adore her, worship her. Of course there is the added attraction of one million gold coins – but I'm sure it is Taloola that the princes are really after.'

'Of course,' murmured Belinda. 'But what about Gordon the goatherd?'

'Don't be ridiculous. A duke's daughter can't marry a goatherd.'

'Why not?'

'Why not? I'll tell you why not. Because er, er . . . they smell! That's why not.'

'Everybody smells,' Belinda pointed out.

'Ah yes, but um, er . . . they've got horns!' cried Dudless. Belinda shook her head.

'No, Uncle: a goat has horns, not a goatherd.'

'Well it's just not done. Ladies in our family always marry princes,' he blustered.

'I didn't. I married an artist.'

'Splrrrrrrrrrgh!' The Duke of Dork almost choked. 'My daughter will marry a prince,' he shouted. Then his face crumpled. 'I can't wait for her to leave home. She's so –

overwhelming, so moody and mountainous. I can't cope any more, and her mother never listens to anything except cheese. Then this dreadful MoNsta appeared – it really is terrible you know – and we all thought we were going to die. In fact I did die, but then my butler woke me up with a cup of tea and said I'd been asleep. And then I got this idea and it really is rather clever you see, because all these princes have arrived here, and they've got to kill the MoNsta and marry Taloola, and then they'll take her away and everything will be peaceful once more.'

Belinda and Hubert and the Bogle were by this time sitting at the Duke's feet, listening

intently to his tale of woe.

'Why can't Gordon the goatherd fight the MoNsta and then marry Taloola?' asked Hubert.

'Oh I don't think that would work at all,' said Dudless. 'Have you met Gordon? He's a vegetarian. Built like a stick insect. He couldn't hurt a fly.'

'Then why not let us deal with the MoNsta?' suggested Belinda. 'And if we get rid of this dreadful MoNsta then Taloola can marry Gordon and everyone will be happy.'

The Duke of Dork brightened visibly for a moment. Then his face fell. 'What about all the princes that have already arrived. I can't just send them away.'

'Don't worry,' said Hubert. 'Belinda and Knackerleevee will deal with the MoNsta long before the princes get anywhere near it. Then Taloola can marry Gordon and leave home, and everyone will be happy ever after. How's that?'

Dudless remained cheerful this time, and the three friends could see that their little adventure was going to be fairly straightforward after all. Unfortunately though, they had rather underestimated the skill and determination of a certain Prinz Blippenbang.

Prinz Blippenbang was a typical handsome prince. He was stunningly strong and good-looking. He had blue eyes, blond hair, a firm, jutting jaw, a straight back and broad shoulders.

He had a powerful chest that rippled with muscles, and even more rippling muscles down each arm and leg.

All these things made him sound too good to be true, and of course he was too good to be true. In fact, he wasn't good at all. He was bad through and through. Here are just a few of the things that Prinz Blippenbang had done in the past.

He had stolen his grandmother's ear-trumpet, filled it with rice pudding and given it back. She almost died of shock when she found rice pudding pouring out of her ear – she thought her brain was falling out of her head.

He had almost drowned his little sister's tortoise in the palace pond by making a submarine out of cardboard and using the tortoise as a test pilot. The submarine sank at once and the tortoise only managed to escape by kicking the sides to bits.

He had frittered away most of his father's fortune by placing bets on such strange things as: 'A fairy-godmother will arrive on Tuesday morning and turn all your pyjamas into gold' or, 'It will rain every day for two hundred years, starting tomorrow.' He could never resist a bet, no matter how ridiculous.

Now Prinz Blippenbang had run out of money altogether, and he was desperate to get his hands on Taloola's fortune, but not on Taloola herself. The Prinz was shrewd and clever. He knew that there would be other princes after the money and, more importantly, he knew that the MoNsta was not going to be an easy victim. MoNstas that eat armies and pet rabbits are not the sort of MoNstas to go all weak at the knees and start begging for mercy if you simply point a sword at them. No, this MoNsta was going to be TROUBLESOME.

And that was why Prinz Blippenbang had brought a bazooka with him.

A bazooka is like a small, portable cannon. It is a very powerful weapon. When the bazooka is loaded and the trigger is pulled something nasty happens. A cannonball comes whizzing out at top speed and flies towards its target in a very dangerous manner. When it hits the target the result is something that looks like a mixture of scrambled egg, tomato sauce and lots of smoke.

Any MoNsta facing a bazooka like the one Prinz Blippenbang had, was going to be in dead trouble. In other words, in trouble and dead. The MoNsta was as good as this already, and he knew it.

When Prinz Blippenbang and all the other princes realized that a girl was going to challenge the MoNsta they almost laughed their socks off. 'But you're a girly!' they cried. 'You can't find the MoNsta!' This was rather stupid of them, but Belinda kept her cool.

'Do you believe in unidentified flying objects?' she asked.

'Of course not,' they scoffed. 'Don't be so silly.'

'I can prove they exist,' said Belinda, smiling. Knowing what was about to happen, Hubert and

Knackerleevee both looked for a safe place to shelter. 'I'll show you,' she said. She waded in amongst the crowd of princes and soon royalties and highnesses were flying right, left and centre. Some flapped their arms like birds, and some whirled round like helicopters, and several made very loud jet noises as they flew through the air.

'Neeeyyaaaaargh!'

The only thing they had in common was that they all crashed with loud thuds and bangs and then limped away moaning and groaning, looking for bandages and sympathy.

Prinz Blippenbang watched with cunning interest as the Karate Princess coolly despatched seventeen princes. Here was someone who might well interfere with his plans. He was going to have to keep a close eye on Belinda and her companions. If he wanted to claim the MoNsta for himself and win those million gold coins, then he would have to do something about the Karate Princess and her friends – like get rid of them.

Prinz Blippenbang patted his bazooka. He was looking forward to putting it into action.

4 The MoNsta Makes a Visit

As Belinda dusted herself down she watched the last of the brave princes crawl away with a pained whimper.

'Can we look yet?' asked Hubert. 'Is it safe?'

'Of course,' laughed Belinda. Knackerleevee banged his hands together.

'You are a warrior, Princessness,' he bellowed cheerfully, but Hubert was more wary.

'I do wish you wouldn't do that. You might at least warn them in advance.'

'What good would that do? They'd just go on laughing and poking fun at me. I hate being made fun of.'

'I'll bear it in mind,' murmured Hubert. 'But maybe you should wear a sign on your jacket – something like: DANGEROUS – DO NOT APPROACH. Anyway, let's get on with the matter in hand. What are we going to do about the MoNsta?'

'We're going to kill it,' declared the Bogle,

making it sound a lot easier than it was going to be.

'How? We're talking about a creature that can fly. It's got two heads and four tongues, which apparently are half a mile long and very sticky. They flick out and things stick to them and then the MoNsta eats them. Big MoNstas with sticky tongues aren't nice, Knackerleevee. I've heard that it's as big as a house.'

'That doesn't mean anything,' the Bogle grumbled. 'What kind of house? It could be a house for a mouse, a mouse-house . . .'

'Don't be silly. Mice don't have hice, I mean houses,' said Hubert. 'You know perfectly well I mean a big house, a proper house.'

Belinda listened to this argument with increasing frustration.

'This isn't getting us anywhere. We need a plan.' But before they could put their heads together loud cries began to ring throughout the castle.

The MoNsta was on the move. It had been seen, hovering over the distant hills and heading towards the castle. Dudless was having a panic attack. It was easy to tell that he was in a state of high anxiety because he was standing on top of the dining table with a paper bag

over his head so that he couldn't see. He was trembling all over, so much so that even the table was quaking. He held a bucket in one hand and he was fiercely brandishing a mop with the other.

'Stand back or I'll shoot!' he yelled. 'You can't get me, you horrible MoNsta!'

'Uncle!' cried Belinda, hurrying into the room. 'It's all right. The MoNsta is still miles away.' The trembling stopped and the mop was lowered.

'Are you sure?' asked the Duke.

'Quite sure. Anyway, you are surrounded by brave princes who have all come here to protect you. Even now some of them are riding out to meet the MoNsta and fight it.'

'Oh? That's a relief.' Dudless pulled the bag off his head. 'Mind you, it won't do any good, Dorinda.'

'BELINDA,' chorused the three friends.

'It will slurp them all up, just like it slurped up my army. It's horrible. Its tongues are all yellow and purple, you know, and slimy.' Hubert helped the Duke down from the table.

'Do you know where it lives?' he asked.

'Afraid not. Nobody knows. Everyone is too scared to follow it. Besides, it flies away. We think it goes off somewhere to sleep after it's eaten, like a snake.'

The Karate Princess frowned. 'This is going to be more difficult than I thought. I was hoping we might be able to catch the beast in its lair, while it's asleep, but if nobody knows where it lives that will be difficult.'

'We can follow it, Highship.'

'We can't fly,' Hubert pointed out.

'I could throw you,' suggested Knackerleevee darkly. He was getting a bit tired of Hubert always being cleverer than he was. He knew he wasn't terribly clever, but he didn't like other people to think so.

Belinda wasn't even listening to them. She had ideas of her own. 'What we need is some string.'

'String? What are you going to do? Tie the MoNsta up?' cried Dudless. 'You can't tie up a MoNsta with little bits of string.' Belinda ignored him.

'I want every bit of string there is in the castle,' she said.

'I think you're very silly,' Dudless replied, stubbornly folding his arms.

Belinda's face darkened. She glanced briefly round the room and her eyes fell upon a big oak armoury cupboard standing at the far end. She approached it slowly, softly and silently. As she drew nearer her whole body became a focus of energy, her muscles tightly sprung. She stopped for a moment, her body coiling itself up, and then she launched her attack. With a few bounds she had thrown herself at the cupboard.

'Haa-akkkk!' Her legs snapped out in front of her and both feet thundered against the cupboard with such force that the doors split apart and the contents spilled out with a noise like a thousand crashing saucepans.

Twelve suits of armour crashed to the floor, followed by helmets and swords and spears and bows and arrows. Finally the cupboard itself teetered forward and crashed to the ground on top of the armour. The Karate Princess turned back to her uncle, eyes blazing.

'I want every bit of

string in the castle,' she repeated. 'Now.'

'No problem,' squeaked the Duke, hurrying off to give the order. 'At once. Your wish is my command.'

'I know I'm not very bright,' muttered the Bogle, 'but why do we need lots of string?'

Belinda sat on the edge of the table. 'It doesn't matter if you are clever or not, Knackerleevee. You are very strong, and a true and trusted friend, and that is more important than being clever.' The Bogle gave Hubert a delighted smirk while Belinda went on.

'I reckon our best hope of defeating the MoNsta is to catch it in its lair, while it's sleeping off one of its heavy meals – do you agree?' The others nodded. 'Our problem is to track the beast down after it has flown away. This may not be a very good idea, and it may not work, but I can't think of anything else at the moment and the pair of you are too busy sniping at each other to be much use. We tie the string together to make one very, very big ball of string and we tie one end of the string to the MoNsta's tail. The MoNsta flies away.

The string unwinds. We hold on to the other end of the string and when the MoNsta goes to sleep we follow the string until we find it.'

Once again the Bogle went into raptures of delight, even kissing Belinda on the forehead. 'You are so clever, Highboat!' Hubert sighed and gave his wife a pale smile.

'Suppose we run out of string while the MoNsta is still flying?'

'Suppose we don't?'

'And how do we tie string on to the tail of a horrible man-eating MoNsta without it knowing?'

Belinda jumped down from the table.

'Don't be so negative, Hubert. I've already said it might not work. Look, I'll do the string-on-the-tail bit, if you're scared.'

'I'm not scared for me,' Hubert said. 'I'm scared for you. We only got married a few days ago, and here you are putting your life in danger.'

The princess's face softened and she hugged Hubert closely, while Knackerleevee turned rather red, gave the pair a soppy grin and sighed.

'Aaaaah. That's so sweet.'

But this touching scene was rudely
interrupted by an ear-piercing scream. 'The
MoNsta is here! It's outside the castle walls!
Pull up the drawbridge! Pull the curtains! Hide
under your beds!'

The three companions rushed over to the
window, and there was the MoNsta in full view.

They stared in
silent awe, until at
last Hubert spoke.

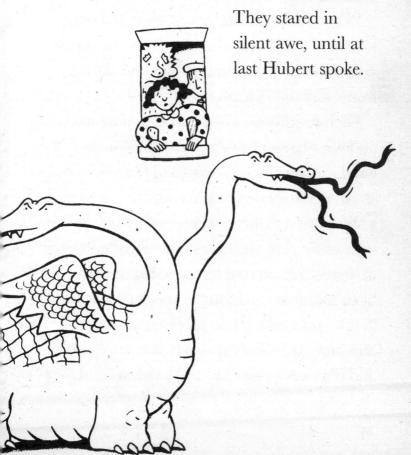

'That is a big MoNsta,' he whispered fearfully.

It was like a brontosaurus, but its skin was scaly, like a crocodile. Its legs were very short and stout, so that its belly trailed upon the ground, crushing anything beneath. Two large wings sprouted from its back. They were folded against its sides, but as the beast darted forward its wings spread and cracked the air with stiff blows.

Behind the MoNsta its tail stretched out, long and scaly, whipping angrily from side to side. And most fearsome of all were its two heads and four tongues.

Each head was on the end of a long neck, and was shaped like that of a giant snake. Cold, unblinking eyes glistened fiercely as it scanned the countryside for food – a cow here, a sheep there, a brave prince or two, complete with horse – all were suddenly engulfed by one of the four flickering tongues. Hubert had been told that each tongue was half a mile long – this was a bit of an exaggeration, although they certainly gave that impression, and if you happened to be the person stuck to the tongue, you probably wouldn't care if it was half a mile long or only a few centimetres.

'That is nasty,' muttered Knackerleevee. Belinda's heart sank. For the first time in her life she felt utterly defeated. This was a MoNsta from hell.

The Duke of Dork came striding back into the room, followed by several servants clutching masses of string. 'I've brought your string Dorinda,' he announced cheerfully. 'I say, what are you all staring at?'

The others made way for Dudless as he came to the window. He peered out, took one look at the MoNsta and slid to the floor.

'I know just how he feels,' murmured Belinda. She could almost hear her own heart screaming at her – 'Let me out! I want to go home!' But she told herself to be strong and began work on the string. 'Come on. Let's get this lot tied together. There's no time to lose.'

From a dark doorway Prinz Blippenbang's eyes narrowed. This was going so well! That silly little girl

could do all the work and lead him to the
MoNsta, then he could take over with his
trusty bazooka.

5 How to Play 'Pin the Tail on the MoNsta'

In the castle courtyard an astonishing scene was taking place. At least forty princes (and for some reason many of them were wearing large plasters or bandages) were pulling on their shining armour. On went the breastplates. On went the metal shoes and leggings, and finally the heavy helmets.

They climbed on to their horses, who were themselves decked out in armour and coloured robes. The princely knights grabbed their lances and spears and swords and shields and generally armed themselves to the hilt with as many weapons as they could carry. They were ready to do battle.

'Lower the drawbridge!' they cried.

Chains banged and rattled through stone channels and with a creak and a groan the great iron drawbridge came clanking down across the moat. A moment later it echoed to the sound of horses' hooves as the valiant

princes rode out to do battle with the MoNsta.
Behind them all came Belinda and Hubert and
the Bogle, carrying no weapons at all except a
very large ball of string.

And behind them came Prinz Blippenbang,
clutching his trusty bazooka.

The brave princes formed a miniature army,
and they went charging towards the MoNsta,
lances at the tilt. Meanwhile, the three
companions, still being shadowed by the Prinz,
made a wide detour, in a bid to get beyond and

behind the fearsome creature.

The princes did not seem to have much of a strategy for attacking the MoNsta. They would rush at it headlong, but as soon as a slurpy tongue came anywhere near them they would turn tail and gallop away screaming. Belinda watched all this from a comfortable distance.

'It's like watching two-year-olds on the beach running away from the waves,' she observed. Nevertheless she was worried. 'I do wish that horrible beast would keep its tail still.'

'You'll have to come with me,' she told the Bogle. 'You might just be strong enough to hold down the end of its tail long enough for me to tie on one end of the string.'

'Not even Knackerleevee is that strong,' Hubert pointed out.

'Don't argue with me, Hubert,' snapped Belinda. 'I need somebody's help out there.

Apart from anything else, someone is going to have to put their finger on the knot so that I can tie it tightly.'

'Put their finger on the knot!' Hubert almost burst out laughing, but he saw the angry look on Belinda's face and wisely kept quiet.

The Bogle grabbed the ball of string and quietly padded after the princess as she began to creep up behind the MoNsta, whose tail was thrashing and crashing about like a shark out of water. This was certainly going to be a tricky operation.

Belinda ran quickly from one hiding place to another, trying to keep an eye on both the MoNsta's heads at once. She approached from the left and then, just as she was tiptoeing up to the tail – PROYYOINNGGG! Up in the air it went and came crashing down in a cloud of dust away to her right.

Belinda approached from the right. She crept towards the MoNsta holding out the string in front of her and was almost there when – WHAANNGGG! Up went the tail again and came down with a tremendous bang

in the centre ground. Belinda approached from
the centre, but didn't even get halfway there
before the tail was off on another sky-bound
journey.

This happened over and over again, until the
Karate Princess finally lost her temper
altogether. 'Oh for goodness sake!'
she bellowed. 'Will you
PLEASE keep still!'
Both heads of the MoNsta
whipped round and four cold
eyes fixed the three friends.
Two mouths opened. Two
horrible hisses came from each
throat and out shot four tongues, like purple
and yellow whips.

'Uh-oh!' cried
Belinda, and
hastily
ran away
so fast that she
overtook both
Knackerleevee
and Hubert. They

threw themselves behind a large rock and lay there panting, while the tips of four tongues writhed about the ground nearby, searching.

'Temper, temper,' muttered Hubert reproachfully.

'I know, I know.' Belinda had to agree with him. She knew her temper was her weak point. When she had been a karate student her teacher – the famous Hiro Ono – had often told her to shut her mind to her temper. 'Lose your temper and lose the battle,' he used to tell her. And just now he had almost been proved right.

Knackerleevee peered out from behind the rock. 'It's gone,' he said. 'I think the MoNsta has found something more interesting. The Bogle was quite right for, over the far hill, attracted by all the noise, came a herd of curious goats, closely followed by their goatherd, Gordon.

The goats had bells hanging from their necks, and they made a pleasant ding-dong noise as they trotted down the hillside. The MoNsta seemed very attracted to the noise too,

because it had
turned away from its search
for Belinda and her friends, and was
now gazing with immense pleasure at the
sight of dinner trotting straight towards it.

Gordon of course was going frantic. 'Come
back you daft animals. That's the MoNsta! It's
not a vegetarian like me! It will have you all for
dinner!' But his shouts were in vain. On went
the goats, bleating merrily, while the MoNsta
became intently quiet. It crouched down on its
great belly, breathing as quietly as possible. Its
four tongues lay curled up and ready, and its
tail lay as still as a dead python.

'Now's our chance,' whispered Belinda.
'Come on, Knackerleevee.' They came out
from behind their rock and began the long

53

creep forward. It seemed to take ages, but still the MoNsta had all its attention fixed firmly on Gordon's goats, who were wandering ever closer. Belinda urged herself on, she had to get the string on the tail before the MoNsta went into action, or realized what was happening at its rear.

At last Belinda was standing right by the tail-tip, and even though it was the tip it was still almost as big as Belinda herself. She grasped the end of the string and gently wound it round and round. She tied a knot. 'Quick, put your finger there,' she ordered, and Knackerleevee dutifully obliged.

Maybe the goats had just got within range, or maybe the MoNsta felt the Bogle's long, sharp nails, but suddenly the tail rose in the air, with Belinda and the Bogle still clinging to it. The MoNsta roared and hissed and the four tongues shot out.

'Blaaaah!' bleated the goats.

'Raaaargh!' hissed the MoNsta.

'Yaaaargh!' yelled Belinda and Knackerleevee.

Down came the tail with a bone-crunching bang. Knackerleevee rolled away into the bushes half-conscious, but Belinda managed to soak up most of the fall with a well-timed judo roll. She sprang to her feet and grabbed the ball of string. The MoNsta already had a mouthful of fresh goat. Poor Gordon the goatherd was in despair, but there was nothing he could do except make sure that he didn't go the same way as his goats. Even the knights in shining armour had run away back to the castle when they saw the fate of the goats. Only Prinz Blippenbang remained, peering out from a large bush. Prinz Blippenbang could feel his ultimate triumph creeping closer and closer.

With a last slurp the MoNsta smiled cheerfully and spread its great wings. They beat the air and the huge beast slowly lifted from the ground. It rose into the air like some monstrous thunder cloud, higher and higher, with the knotted string trailing out behind, and then it flew away, accompanied by the faint sound of muffled goats' bells. Belinda unrolled the string as fast as she could. Hubert ran over and began helping.

'Are you all right?' he cried. 'I thought that was the end of you when you were whisked up in the air like that.'

'I'm OK. Just keep unwinding the string and pray that it doesn't break.'

Knackerleevee groaned and staggered to his feet.

'Urgh – I feel as if I've just been hurled to the ground by a monstrous tail.'

'Help us unwind the string!' they both shouted and he hurried over. The ball was rapidly dwindling and the MoNsta had almost vanished from view.

'We're going to run out of string!' yelled Belinda, as the last piece ran through her fingers. She grabbed the end before it could be whisked away and she was off, half running, half jumping as she tried to keep up with the MoNsta's flight.

And then all at once the string went slack. Belinda stood on the hillside panting furiously, still clutching the string, while the others ran to catch up with her.

'You've still got it!' cried Hubert with admiration.

'Yes, but have I got it because the MoNsta has settled down to sleep, or because the string has snapped somewhere?'

'There's only one way to find out,' Hubert pointed out, but before they could set off they were suddenly confronted by a groaning Gordon, grieving for his goats.

'All my goats! Every single one! Gobbled up, like . . . like . . . goats that have been gobbled, I suppose.'

'You have a lovely way with words,' murmured Hubert.

'I'm in shock,' cried Gordon. 'My goats have been gobbled.'

'Pull yourself together,' Belinda ordered.

'What would Taloola say if she saw you like this?'

Gordon gave a mighty sniff.

'You're right. I must pull myself together.' He gazed with curiosity at the length of string in Belinda's hand.

'Where's the balloon?' he asked.

'There isn't a balloon on the end of this string,' Belinda explained. 'There's a MoNsta, at least we hope that is what is on the end, because we intend to follow the string to the MoNsta's lair and then we shall kill it before it can do any more damage.'

'Then I must come with you!' cried Gordon, 'so that I can see that justice is done, for the sake of my goats.'

With that they began following the string.

Not so very far behind them Prinz Blippenbang emerged from behind his rock and began discreetly to follow the MoNsta hunters.

'I'm coming too,' he muttered quietly, 'because where Belinda goes, I go, but what Belinda does I shall claim I did myself. Then I shall have the money and Taloola. I shall keep the money of course, but Taloola can jump off a cliff for all I care. Hee hee hee!'

6 The Princess in the Pothole

The string led them over the first hill and on to the brow of the second hill where for the first time they were able to see a long cliff face beyond. In front of them the string stretched out through the air.

'There must be a cave or something in the cliff,' mused Hubert. He set off at a run down the hill and across a narrow gully until he reached the bottom of the cliff. 'Look, up beyond that big clump of bushes. Isn't that a hole?'

Belinda and the Bogle squinted up to where Hubert was pointing. Then they saw it – a long, dark fissure in the rock, half hidden by bushes.

'It's just about big enough for the MoNsta to crawl through,' she murmured, 'and if it's big enough for the MoNsta then it's certainly big enough for us.'

'It's much bigger inside,' Gordon

announced. Belinda looked
round, startled.

'Really? How do you
know?'

'One of my nanny
goats went in there
last year. She'd hurt
her leg and couldn't
climb down. I had
to rescue her.'
Gordon sniffed
loudly. 'Now she's back
in there again, only this
time she's gone for ever.
My poor little goats.' He
snuffled again and
hastily wiped away a
tear with his wispy
beard.

'Come on,' said Belinda.
'It's no use crying over
spilled goats' milk. Let's get up there and find
the MoNsta.' Gordon nodded bravely and they
began to climb.

61

The cliff face was crumbly, but at least there were plenty of hand and foot holds, and they were soon well on their way to the opening. Knackerleevee made the mistake of looking down to see how far they had come.

'Ohohoh,' he moaned. 'It's a long way down, Nestship. Oooh, I don't like it. My knees are going wobbly and my stomach feels like a bowl of very sloppy yoghurt.'

'Don't look down,' said Hubert. 'Keep your eye on the cave-mouth. Come on.' He held out a helping hand and gently guided the great creature higher. Once again Belinda was touched at Hubert's care and kindness. I don't deserve him, she thought. He's too kind. But of course she did deserve him really, and she looked after him in her own way, so they were well suited. They reached the hole in the rock and hauled themselves over the edge. 'Phwooor!' cried Hubert, holding his nose. 'This place stinks!' A revolting smell of old cabbage and boiled eggs drifted from the mouth of the cave.

'Ssssh, you'll wake the MoNsta,' whispered the princess and she tiptoed forward, following the string. The cave was very dark and they paused for a few moments until their eyes grew used to the lack of light, but even then they could hardly see a thing. As they pressed deeper into the cave the smell became ever more powerful and they clenched their hands over their faces.

Some distance behind them, and keeping well out of sight, Prinz Blippenbang darted from rock to rock as he carefully tailed the four MoNsta hunters.

Gordon was right about the size of the cave. The roof quickly soared higher and higher. The place was like a gigantic hall. Fat stalagmites sat dotted about the floor like grumpy old men, fast asleep. From the ceiling long thin stalactites were still dripping with water.

'It's so beautiful,' whispered Hubert. 'I wish I could stop and paint it all. It would make a wonderful picture.'

'I think we ought to sort out this beastie thing first,' Belinda answered. 'We're almost there. Keep very, very quiet.'

They rounded a big outcrop of rock and there in front of them was the MoNsta, fast asleep. It had a peaceful smile on both of its faces and it was breathing quietly and slowly, its great belly heaving up and down. The string was still tied round the end of its tail. A strange smoke seemed to drift away from the beast as it lay there, as if it was smouldering. But it wasn't smoke – it was pure MoNsta pong. The horrible odour rose from the body in great wafts and clung in the air.

Hubert turned to Knackerleevee. 'I used to think you smelled a bit sometimes, but this is the stink to end

all stinks.' The Bogle grunted. He was not sure if Hubert had said something nice or not.

For almost five minutes the companions just stood and gazed at the sleeping hulk, overwhelmed by the sheer size of the beast. Finally they withdrew a little and crouched down behind a large stalagmite.

'What's the plan?' asked Knackerleevee.

Belinda raised a cross eyebrow. 'Do I have to think of everything? My idea was the string-thing. Now it's somebody else's turn to think. My brain's having a rest.'

The Bogle and Hubert gazed at each other. Neither of them had a weapon, and the MoNsta was far too big to manhandle in any way at all. They were filled with deep depression – to have risked life and limb to get this far and then find they couldn't kill the beast! It was monstrous!

Gordon the goatherd was standing up and leaning across the side of the stalagmite, staring intently at the MoNsta. He seemed to have overcome his grief, and now anger was taking over. His bony fingers gripped the edge of the stalagmite like fierce talons. His dark eyes were hard and shining and they fixed the beast with murderous intent.

'That horrible heap ate my goats,' he hissed. 'It ate Mirabel and Flossy and Duncan and Bert and Barnaby and little Trixie and, and . . . every single one of them.'

'Don't think about that now,' said Belinda softly, alarmed by Gordon's rising voice. 'Sit down and help us think of a plan to get rid of it.'

But Gordon pulled his arm away and hissed back at her through grimly gritted teeth. 'I don't need a plan. That goat-gobbler is a murderer!' With this final cry Gordon pulled a short sword from his belt and strode straight for the beast.

'Stop – you'll be killed!' warned Hubert, but Gordon carried on.

It was truly pitiful, and it made the three companions want to weep. Gordon had no chance at all. He was a thin, scrawny man with nothing except a sword in his hand and anger in his heart, yet here he was marching on the beast. Belinda and Hubert and Knackerleevee held their breath. They almost stopped breathing altogether as they watched with mounting horror and fascination.

Every so often the MoNsta would flick open one eye. It was impossible to say where it would look. Sometimes Gordon nipped behind a pile of bones. Sometimes he just froze, as if he were one of the stalagmites in the cave. And somehow he managed to creep closer and closer.

The MoNsta flicked open an eye and stirred. It let out a thunderous belch and then slumped back into a doze again. Gordon took three more steps and now he stood right beside one of the huge heads. It was revolting. The scales were dull and flecked with blood. From the slit of a mouth several teeth poked out and some still had bits of goat fur stuck to them. Gordon's rage seized hold of him, giving him the power of ten men. He raised his sword above his head, grasping the solid handle with

both hands, and plunged it
down into the MoNsta's
skull.

The great neck and
head twitched,
throwing Gordon to
one side, but he was
up on his feet again,
running furiously to
the second head,
which was
stirring into
wakefulness. But
before the MoNsta
could react
Gordon had straddled the beast's neck, raised
his sword a second time and dispatched the
beast for ever. The MoNsta gave a huge groan,
lifted its second head for a last time and
crashed to the ground.

'Incredible!' whispered Belinda, her face
flushed with admiration. 'You've killed the
MoNsta, Gordon. Well done!'

The friends crowded round the goatherd,

patting him on the back, ruffling his hair and tweaking his beard. Gordon however felt flat and exhausted. All the fight had gone out of him, and now that he realized what danger he had been in he suddenly felt scared, even though there was nothing left to be scared about.

'This is excellent,' declared Belinda. 'Gordon has killed the MoNsta, so Gordon wins Taloola's hand and the million gold coins. What could be better?'

A deep voice from the far end of the cave surprised them all. 'Oh, I have a much better ending,' said Prinz Blippenbang.

'What? Who's that? Come out of the shadows,' cried Belinda, already bristling with a premonition that further danger was afoot.

The Prinz took several steps forward, his bazooka balanced over one shoulder and pointing at the friends. 'Allow me to introduce myself. I am Prinz Blippenbang and I have come to claim the MoNsta's heads. So kind of you all to lead me here, and even kinder of you to kill it for me. I do so hate getting my hands

dirty. Don't move a muscle!' he cried as
Belinda took a couple of angry steps towards
him. 'This is a bazooka, a very powerful
weapon, and you will do exactly as I say. You
there!' The Prinz gestured at Gordon. 'Goat-
boy! Cut off the MoNsta's heads, put them in
these sacks and bring them to me. Hurry!'

Gordon could only do as he was told while
the others watched in stunned silence. The
heads were stuffed into the sacks and laid at
Blippenbang's feet. The Prinz grabbed them
with his free hand and laughed loudly. 'I am
going to enjoy myself,' he
bragged. 'I shall go back to the
castle and tell that stupid
pumpkin of a Duke what a
terrible battle I had. I shall
show him the heads and
he will be so
pleased! Then
he'll give me a
million gold coins
and I shall be rich for ever!'

'What about Taloola?' cried Gordon.

'Oh hang Taloola! Taloola's a fat, ugly tub.'

'No she isn't! She's the most beautiful woman I have ever laid eyes on!' Gordon declared.

'Oh do shut up, you grubby goat-goon.' The Prinz began to back out of the cave. 'I'm sorry I have to dash off now, but unfortunately, because you all know the truth of what has happened here, I must leave you behind. I shall tell the Duke how the MoNsta had crunched you up in front of my very eyes before I could kill it.'

'You're not going to kill us are you?' Hubert had turned very pale.

'Um . . . not exactly. However, I would so much like to show you how powerful my bazooka is, so I am going to fire it at the cave roof here. The roof will come tumbling down and what a tragedy, you'll be trapped, for ever. What a shame. Boo hoo.'

'You're a monster!' cried Belinda. 'Worse than the MoNsta monster!'

'You say such nice things,' replied Blippenbang sweetly. 'Oh well, I really must be going. So nice to have met you.'

With that the Prinz backed away to the entrance, turned his bazooka on the cave roof and pulled the trigger. Flames shot from the cannon. There was a deafening bang and moments later rocks began cascading down. Big boulders, little boulders, stalagmites that had taken thousands of years to grow, all came crashing down. They piled up at the entrance, rapidly rising, blocking out what little daylight there was until – nothing. Just darkness.

'Oh dear,' muttered the Karate Princess. 'I think we're trapped.'

7 Rabbits and Other Revelations

'Can you see anything?' asked Knackerleevee.

'No,' grumbled the others.

'Neither can I. Thank goodness.'

'What do you mean – "thank goodness"?'
Hubert snapped. 'We're trapped halfway up a
mountain in a deep cave, with no food and in
total darkness. Why are you thanking
goodness?'

'Because I thought I might have gone blind,
but if nobody can see then I know that it's just
got a bit darker.' The Bogle stumbled forwards,
feeling his way with waggling, hairy fingers.

'Oi!' cried the goatherd. 'Watch where
you're putting your great hairy hands. That
was my bottom, if you don't mind.'

'Sorry,' muttered Knackerleevee. He took a
step back, tripped over Belinda, tumbled
backwards and sent Hubert sprawling, before
finally falling flat on his face himself. The cave
rang with angry and painful cries. It got even

worse as they struggled to their feet, reaching out, hitting others accidentally and knocking them down again.

'Stop!' cried Belinda. 'Just keep still – everyone! This darkness is hopeless. Let's just all sit down where we are, one by one. Hubert – sit down.'

'I'm sitting.'

'Gordon, sit.'

'I'm not a dog,' complained the goatherd.

'SIT! Knackerleevee, you sit down next, and now me. There, no accidents. Right, we are in a very nasty situation. Has anyone got any ideas as to how we get out?'

'If we feel around we could find the string and follow it to the entrance,' suggested the Bogle. 'Then we might be able to move the rocks out of the way.'

'Hmmm. I think the rock-pile brought down by Blippenbang is far too dense. It would take weeks to get through, and we haven't got weeks. Hubert – any ideas?'

'I agree with Knackerleevee.'

'You do?' The Bogle was definitely surprised to hear this.

'The way we came in is the only way in, so it must be the only way out,' Hubert said logically. 'We shall simply have to dig for our lives.'

'OK, it's agreed then.' Belinda nodded. 'Get down on your hands and knees and try and find the string.'

'You haven't asked me yet,' Gordon

muttered sulkily.

'Oh, sorry. Gordon! Have you got an idea?' asked Belinda brightly and waited for him to say 'No'. She knew he was angry with her for shouting at him.

'Yes, I have, and it's better than your idea too.'

'What is it?'

'Why should I tell you?' he asked sulkily.

'Because if you don't we shall all die in this cave with nothing but a stinking dead MoNsta for company and Prinz Blippenbang will get the money that you deserve AND he'll get Princess Taloola and he doesn't love her like you do and she'll be so unhappy she'll probably never eat again and pine away to nothing and die.'

'That'll take a long time,' remarked Knackerleevee darkly, and promptly received a kick from the princess. 'Sorry,' he added.

'All right, I'll tell you,' said Gordon. 'At the back of this cave there is a narrow passage that leads to the top of the cliff. That's how I managed to rescue my goat.'

'You mean there's another way out?!'

'Yes.'

'Why didn't you tell us?' cried Hubert.

'I just have.'

'But I thought you climbed up here from the bottom.'

'No, I never said that. I climbed down here from the top.'

'Surely we should be able to see a chink of daylight if there's a passageway to the top?' asked Belinda.

'The MoNsta's tail is blocking it off,' said Gordon. 'I'll lead the way. We shall have to hold each other's feet so that we don't lose contact.'

So Knackerleevee held on to Hubert's ankles, and Hubert held on to Belinda's ankles, and she held on to the goatherd's ankles, and off they went, like a choo-choo train, puffing and grunting and hissing with effort. It did not take them long to reach the MoNsta's tail, and with a lot of one, two, three and HEAVE! they pushed the tail out of the way and revealed a narrow, perpendicular chink of light.

'Gordon – you are very clever,' announced Belinda. 'Let's get going, and let's hope that we are not too late.'

Dudless, Duke of Dork didn't know whether to laugh or cry. 'The MoNsta's dead! No more weeping and wailing. No more danger. No more hiding in paper bags. Oh, but poor Dorinda – what a way to go. Crunched to bits, you say?' Prinz Blippenbang nodded.

'I tried my best to save them, but . . .' He looked suitably upset. The Duke patted the Prinz on one shoulder.

'There, there. Everyone knew the risk they were taking, eh? I shall write to my brother and let him know. Poor Dorinda.' The Duke was silent for a few moments and then he brightened up a bit. 'But you're alive! That is good news. Do you know? I think I'm going to treat myself to a new pet rabbit. And what shall I call him?' The Duke's gaze rested fondly on his new-found hero, the wonderful MoNsta-masher, Prinz Blippenbang. 'I shall call him Bloppenpop, after you!'

'How kind,' said the Prinz, smiling. 'Now, about those million gold coins . . .'

'All in good time, dear thing, all in good time. I expect you want to be with the blushing bride. Taloola, do stop snivelling and snuffling. Look what a fine prize you have here. Prinz Bloppenpop is so strong, and handsome.'

'I loved Gordon the goatherd. He was sweet and kind and had a wispy beard that tickled and now he's dead and gone and I shall never be happy again. Ohwohwoh!' And she burst into tears and threw herself on the settee.

'She'll get over it, dear chap,' said the Duke cheerfully.

'About the money . . .' hinted the Prinz again.

'Yes indeed, all in good time, but we must have a wedding, and a wotchamacallit, you know, where everyone goes round . . .'

'Merry-go-round?' suggested the Prinz.

'No, no, everyone goes round and they do

things with their feet . . . a football, no, that doesn't sound quite right. It's on the tip of my tongue you know.'

'Do you mean a ball,' suggested Blippenbang. 'Where everyone dances?'

'That's it! That's it. What a clever chappie you are. Brains and muscles eh? Yes, we must have a Grand Ball tonight to celebrate the Defeat of the MoNsta, and then the wedding and your million gold coins.'

Prinz Blippenbang smiled politely. 'Lovely idea, but I don't suppose I could have the money before the wedding?'

'No, no, that will be my wedding present,' said the Duke. 'Surely you don't expect me to give you a million gold coins and a wedding present? That would be greedy! Now, do excuse me Bloppenpop, I must go and organize the ball.'

Prinz Blippenbang ground his teeth together and watched the stout little Duke hurry away. What a stupid man he was. So, he would have to marry Taloola before he got the money? Oh well, no matter. He would just have to ditch her after the wedding instead of before it. He went to his room to prepare for the dance.

To be fair to the Duke it must be admitted that he pulled out all the stops for the Grand Ball. The entire castle was decked out with flowers and balloons and a huge feast had been prepared. Everyone was invited. Ladies pulled out their finest gowns and the castle was filled from cellars to attics with laughter and song and relief and joy that they were out of danger at last.

Only two people were not sharing in the merry-making. Taloola moped about the hall with tears streaming down her puffed-up face. Meanwhile Prinz Blippenbang tugged on his best dancing jacket. He was wondering how quickly he could get the money from the Duke.

The band arrived and set up at one end of the great hall. Music rose into the air with a twirl and a flourish and soon numerous feet were skipping and turning and twirling and bouncing as the excited guests danced their socks off.

Outside in the fragrant evening, four weary travellers hurried towards the sound of music and the glittering lights of the celebrating castle. 'I do hope we're not too late,' said Hubert. 'Come on Knackerleevee, hurry up.'

'I've got a stitch,' complained the Bogle, sitting on the ground and clutching one side. 'You go on. I'll catch you up.'

Belinda and the others hurried back to him. 'You two take his arms. I'll take his legs. Come on.'

Before the Bogle could protest he found himself being carried at a trot towards the castle, bouncing up and down like a big piece of carpet. When they arrived at the drawbridge they were met by several guards brandishing crossed spears.

'We want to go inside,' declared Belinda.

'Oh yes? Where's your invitation?'

'You're not even wearing a ball gown,'

sneered a second guard.

'I haven't got a ball gown,' said Belinda.

'There you go then. You can't come in. And pick that bit of carpet up before you leave.'

'This is becoming very boring,' warned Belinda. 'Are you going to let us through or not?'

'Definitely not,' said the third guard, smiling.

'I think you ought to do as she asks,' said Hubert helpfully. 'Otherwise she might do something rather unpleasant.'

'Ooh, we are scared!' cried the guards.

'What's she going to do? Blow a raspberry!'

Hubert and Knackerleevee covered their eyes. Gordon, who had never seen the Karate Princess in action, 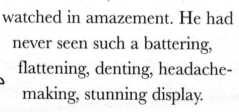 watched in amazement. He had never seen such a battering, flattening, denting, headache-making, stunning display.

'Ha-akk!' cried Belinda as she made mincemeat of the three guards, and cast them one by one into the cold, wet moat below. 'Happy fishing!' she cried as she crossed the drawbridge and marched into the great hall. She went straight up to the dance band, grabbed the biggest drum she could find and banged it and banged it until the music stopped, the dancers stopped, and all eyes were on her.

Prinz Blippenbang was visibly shaken and now Belinda pointed an accusing finger at him. 'Uncle, that man is a cheat, and a would-be murderer. He's about as much a hero as a jar of jam.'

The Duke was in a tizzy. He could make no sense at all of what was happening. 'Um, Dorinda, you're dead, aren't you? What are you doing here? And what kind of jam were you thinking of?'

'Uncle! It doesn't matter about any jam and I'm not dead, even though the Prinz tried to kill me and my friends. He's claiming that he killed the MoNsta, but he didn't. He was too scared to go anywhere near the beast.'

This pronouncement really set tongues wagging. The brave Prinz not brave at all? What was going on? And where was the Prinz anyway?

Blippenbang was no fool. He could see the way things were going. But he was determined not to lose out on the million gold coins. He raced up the stairs to his room to fetch his trusty bazooka.

8 And Did They All Live Happily Ever After?

Prinz Blippenbang burst into his room, but someone had beaten him to it.

'Looking for something?' asked Hubert, pointing the bazooka at the cursing Prinz. 'I think we had better go back downstairs, don't you? You go first.' Blippenbang had no alternative but to head back down the stairs, looking thunderous.

'Will somebody please tell me what's going on?' squeaked the Duke when he saw the Prinz being escorted into the hall. Belinda explained, recounting the whole story, from the moment they set off to fasten the string to the MoNsta's tail, right up until when they got back to the castle. Dudless, Duke of Dork, listened to the tale with growing anger.

'Is this true?' he demanded of the Prinz.

'What if it is?'

'Don't you even love my beautiful daughter?'

'Pah! Beautiful? I'd rather marry a camel!'

At this point Gordon the goatherd almost threw himself on the Prinz, but it was Taloola who held him back. She walked over to the Prinz and gazed up into his blue eyes. 'I may not be a beauty as considered by some people,' she said with great dignity. 'I'm so sorry I displease you, Prinz Blippenbang. Please, excuse me.'

Taloola turned gracefully away, then all at once whirled round and delivered such a stunning slap to the Prinz's face that he staggered back several paces, clutching his cheek. Taloola made the Prinz an elegant curtsy and went back to her admiring goatherd. The dancers cheered and Blippenbang crept away like a bruised snake, thoroughly outwitted and shamed into the bargain.

Dudless was still spluttering with confusion.

'Will somebody please tell me who killed the MoNsta? If it wasn't Bottompop then who was it?'

'Gordon the goatherd!' everyone cried.

'Gordon? But he's a vegetarian. I thought he didn't believe in killing animals.'

'I'm afraid I lost my temper,' said Gordon sheepishly. 'The MoNsta killed all my goats, and I was very angry.'

'Quite so,' said the Duke, patting Gordon on the back affectionately. 'But never mind. We shall get you some more goats and, and rabbits too! Do you like rabbits? I love 'em. I'm going to get a new rabbit, and I shall call it Gordon, after you, my brave little rabbit.' This produced more clapping and cheering, but the Duke hadn't finished.

'Well now, if you killed the MoNsta then you win the prize, and I hope you'll be, ooops, there they go already! There's no stopping young love!' He stepped back hurriedly as Taloola flung herself into Gordon's arms, bearing him backwards at full speed until at last they crashed into the band.

'Ah music!' cried the
Duke. 'That's what we
need, more dancing.
On your feet
everyone! Dorinda,
go and put on one
of the Duchess's

outfits, they should fit you all right. Hubert,
you're fine. Hmmm, I don't know about the
Bogle. A bit of lipstick maybe?'

'I don't think so, Uncle,' laughed Belinda.
'Leave him as he is. Besides, he won't want to
dance. He gets the stitch you know.' She
hurried upstairs to the Duchess's dressing room
and there she found outfits galore. The
Duchess herself was sitting in the corner, doing
a jigsaw puzzle. She seemed only slightly
surprised that Belinda was going through her
best clothes, but was too busy trying to find a
missing jigsaw piece to take the cheese out of
her ears and actually ask what she was doing.

Belinda pulled out the garments one by one
and looked at them. She held them in front of
her and gazed into a mirror. Belinda didn't like

balls. She preferred racing round chipping and chopping and having exciting adventures, but she knew she couldn't do that all the time. She supposed she would have to try on one of the outfits and go back down to the dance.

Belinda chose the best one, pulled it on, sighed and went downstairs. The moment she appeared she was surrounded by handsome princes, all asking for the first dance, but she only had eyes for Hubert.

'You look stunning,' he said, smiling.

'I am stunning,' answered the Karate Princess. 'I do an awful lot of stunning. I stunned those guards outside this evening, if you remember.'

'I do, and now you've stunned me too,' said Hubert, blushing. 'Would you like to dance?' And the happy couple went tripping and crashing and bumping and banging all the way across the dance floor.

The reason for all this crashing and banging was that Belinda was probably the most hopeless dancer in the world. She was excellent at karate. She could speak four different languages. She could make a mean omelette and chips. But dancing was simply not one of her talents. When Belinda went dancing in a crowded ballroom, it was like watching a team of expert tree-fellers at work. You could tell exactly where she was because the other dancers were falling over all around her, like trees in a forest being cut down in one sweep. The other dancers were tripped over by her feet, nudged by her elbows, and toppled by her barging shoulders.

Within a couple of minutes the dance floor was a writhing mass of fallen bodies, and only Hubert and Belinda were still on their feet. 'What's happened to Taloola and Gordon?' asked the princess.

'I think they're busy,' said Hubert, grinning, and pointed across to the dance band. The two lovebirds were sitting surrounded by violin players. They were holding hands and gazing rapturously into each other's eyes. Everyone in the room discreetly turned away and began talking about the weather.

'What a lovely morning!' cried a blushing Duke.

'Uncle, it's almost midnight,' Belinda pointed out.

'Quite so. I must say it's been an excellent day, has it not?'

'It certainly has,' said Hubert. 'We've had a fantastic adventure, not without its hairy bits I might add . . .'

'Oh! You mean the Bogle,' Uncle Dudless said seriously, and everyone burst out laughing.

'What? What did I say? Something funny? Did I make a joke? What was it? Oh, I am a one!'

It was while they were all falling about with laughter that the Duchess of Dork appeared at the top of the grand staircase. She gazed down at the noisy throng below her, as if she'd just found a mouse in her soup.

'I say!' cried the Duchess, plucking the cheese from her ears. 'People have been coming and going for days, and now there's dancing in the hall. What on earth has been going on? Will someone please tell me?'